Karen McCombie
The Mystery of Me

KaRen McCombie
The Mystery of Me

With illustrations by
Cathy Brett

Barrington Stoke

For Daisy Weston (and her fairy godmother, Margaret Sawkins, who made this happen!)

First published in 2017 in Great Britain by
Barrington Stoke Ltd
18 Walker Street, Edinburgh, EH3 7LP

www.barringtonstoke.co.uk

Text © 2017 Karen McCombie
Illustrations © 2017 Cathy Brett

The moral right of Karen McCombie and Cathy Brett to be
identified as the author and illustrator of this work has been
asserted in accordance with the Copyright, Designs and
Patents Act, 1988

A CIP catalogue record for this book is available
from the British Library upon request

ISBN: 978-1-78112-720-9

Printed in China by Leo

Contents

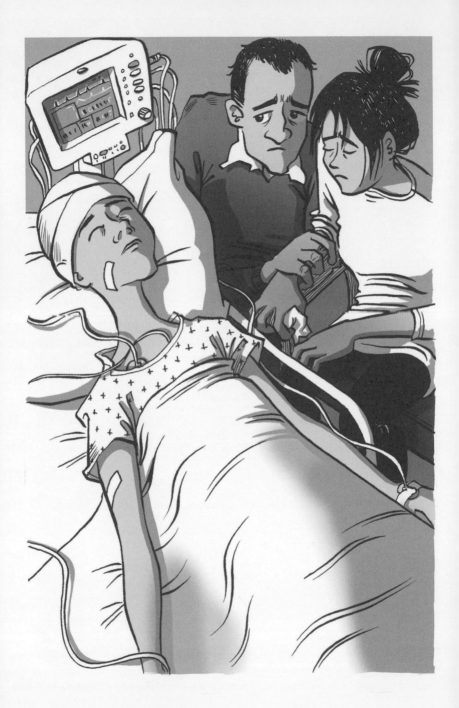

Chapter 1

The same old Ketty?

I can't remember dying.

But it was only for two minutes, 39 seconds. Then the paramedics got my heart started again.

I can't remember the crash, or anything about the two weeks after it. That's no surprise, since I was in a coma.

I lay lost in some strange, deep sleep, letting my bruised brain heal, while my poor parents sat beside me. Mum said they stayed by my hospital bed for hour after hour, day after day, holding hands and hoping. Just hoping I'd wake up and be me, their sweet little Ketty.

The doctor tried to warn them that people can seem different after a head injury. A fun-loving person may turn serious. A shy, easy-going person may turn loud and short-tempered. Or maybe – after plenty of rest – there'd be no change at all. It's like the flip of a coin ... and my parents didn't know how that coin would land for me.

Thankfully, I ended up the same old Ketty, they say.

Not that I'm sure who the old Ketty is ... That's pretty hazy for me too, same as the crash.

I've been off school the last couple of months, and my memory is creeping back in scraps and wisps. Faces, places, people – they pop into my mind at odd times. I was having a bowl of tomato soup at the kitchen table when a sudden image came to me. It was a big, noisy room, packed with teenagers, talking and eating.

"The school canteen!" Mum said when I described it.

The first time Mum and Dad took me for a walk in the park, I looked at the children's playground and I remembered sitting on the swings. The sway of them, the thick, cold links of metal in my hands, the giggles of girls beside me.

"That must have been Adele and Urmi! Your best friends!" Dad said.

I've only seen Adele and Urmi one time since the crash, but it felt like it was the first time I'd *ever* met them. When they came to the house we were all a bit shy, and I went stiff when they hugged me. I smiled and nodded as they spoke about teachers and kids at school who sent their love, but the names they said didn't mean anything to me. I couldn't match the names with faces – or even with feelings – at all.

But perhaps today it will happen at last, cos today is my first day back at Heartfield Academy.

"You'll only be here for the morning, Ketty, so you won't get *too* tired," Mum reminds me now, as we walk in the front door of the school.

"OK," I say with a nod, as I stare around me.

I'm pleased to see that I *do* know this place.

The corridor with the grey floor tiles, the blue sofa for visitors, the office with the smiley lady behind the sliding glass window. There are no crowds of kids in here – my parents and the school decided it was best for me to come in after the mad crush at the start of the day at 8.30 a.m.

4

"Hello, Ketty! How nice to see you!" the smiley lady says. She gets up and comes out of a door and into the corridor.

Her name flutters around in my mind like a moth, but I can't seem to catch hold of it. That happens a lot. Even the simplest words are there one second, and gone the next. My doctor says this will get better bit by bit. He says I have to try not to get frustrated when the words fly away out of my grasp.

That's easy for *him* to say.

"Stella!" I shout out too loudly, as the memory moth wafts to the front of my mind.

"Yes, well done!" Stella the receptionist says. She and Mum smile at each other, as if I'm a toddler who has learned a new word.

I was pleased when I remembered, but that look they share makes me feel a bit stupid.

"Now don't worry at all today, Ketty," Stella says. "As you know, everyone has been told you need to take it slow. And everyone knows not to talk about ..."

Stella goes red.

She was about to say "... the crash ..." but she stopped herself.

I suppose she's worried that it'll be too upsetting for me to think about – and awkward for her too.

But, like I say, it's all blank to me.

"Good luck, darling," Mum says, and she gives my arm a little rub. "It'll be fine."

As soon as she waves and leaves, I turn to Stella, who will take me to my first class.

And then I see two girls further up the corridor. Their school shoes have stopped

pitta-patting on the shiny floor and they're staring at me as if I have two heads and three noses. They're whispering madly, hands not quite covering their mouths.

Uh-oh.

Is Mum right? Will I be fine?

I'm not so sure.

Chapter 2

Silent staring

I've been beamed in from Mars.

I've turned blue overnight.

There's a huge neon arrow flashing above my head, pointing down at me.

The way everyone is staring at me, any of those might be true.

Mr Hunter is up at the whiteboard, talking about a poem. No one is listening. One by one, they all turn like nervy meerkats in the desert to sneak a look at me.

Maybe they were expecting my head to be all shaved, with a vivid pink scar and big bumps where my skull had been stapled together.

Instead, I look much the same as I did before the crash, with long dark hair and no scars.

I'm not ready to have all these eyes on me. I'm not good with too much noise – in fact I'm allowed to leave lessons a few minutes early, so I can get to my next class before the bell goes and the crush and chaos start. But these silent stares are freaking me out. I can feel myself getting hotter, I can feel bubbles of panic rise from my tummy into my chest.

"So, can anyone tell me what the image in this line means?" Mr Hunter says, as he turns to face us all.

His eyes land on me. I'm lucky. He can tell I'm on the verge of losing it.

"Do you want to scoot off to your next lesson now, Ketty?" he asks.

It's kind of him. It's *way* before the end of the lesson.

"Thank you, sir," I mutter, and I shove my book and pencil case into my bag and hurry to the door.

Everyone's eyes bore into my back as I leave. When I close the door on them and I'm alone in the long, cool corridor, it feels good.

Only ...

Only I don't know where I'm meant to go next. I scrabble in the top pocket of my blazer and pull out a sheet of paper with my timetable printed on it.

My finger moves along the column.

"Today is Monday," I mumble to myself. "So the second lesson is Maths."

OK, fine. I have solved the problem. Now my *next* problem is how to find the class ...

My eyes are prickling with tears when I hear a voice.

"Ketty? Are you OK?"

I look up and see a friendly face, a warm smile. It's a boy I don't know, but he seems to know *me*. He has a yellow slip in his hand – and I remember that means a pupil has permission to be out of class.

"My next class ... I won't be able to find it," I tell this stranger. "I won't be able to find *any* of them!" I waft the useless timetable around.

The boy takes it from me, stares at it and nods.

"It's cool," he says. "I'll draw you a map of the school so you can get to all your classes." He pulls a book and a pen out of his bag. "It'll be a bit scrappy but it'll do."

The bubbles of panic start to fade away. I take slow, deep breaths as he doodles, and I feel my sense of control come back.

"Thank you," I say. I wish I knew his name.

"No problem, Ketty," he says, and he grins up at me. "And I'm Otis, by the way."

Otis. Otis. *Otis.*

I repeat it in my head in an attempt to fix it in my short-term memory, which can trip me up sometimes.

"Thank you. Thank you, Otis," I repeat, adding the name of my new hero.

Chapter 3

Questions without answers

Day One is done.

I was so tired when I got home from school that I had a nap in the afternoon, and then I went to bed super-early. I think Mum and Dad wanted to ask me all about my day, but I was too quiet. They know that if I'm quiet, it's because my brain is overloaded and I need to rest.

I think they were just glad I made it. I survived my first morning in school and I didn't say that I hated it and never wanted to go back.

Of course, I felt like that a few times in the different lessons, but Otis's map and his kindness sort of held me together.

And now it's Day Two.

It's break-time, and I've been sitting in Learning Support with Adele and Urmi. It's nice and chilled.

They talk away, and I listen and sometimes don't, but it's OK. It feels comfy to be with them, even if I only *know* they're my best friends and don't *feel* that they are.

"Oops! Nearly the end of break," Urmi says, and she looks at the clock on the wall.

"Yeah, let's get you along to the counsellor before the bell goes, Ketty," Adele says. She grabs her bag and stands up.

We walk out of Learning Support and into the corridor, where a few people stand eating snacks or drift along chatting.

Adele and Urmi don't have far to take me – the counsellor's office is just a few doors along. I have it marked on the map Otis did for me.

As soon as I think of Otis, like magic, there he is. He's quite a way away, but I smile and return his wave.

There's no chance for any more than that, cos me, Adele and Urmi are outside the office of the school counsellor.

My two friends say bye and fade away, while I knock-knock and wait.

The counsellor – Maryam – opens the door and ushers me inside.

I'm a bit shy, but I met her before when she came to my house on Friday, so that helps.

She sits me down and says, "Good to see you again, Ketty. So, how's it going so far?" with a cheerful smile.

"It's … OK," I say, not sure how to start.

I've had lots of feelings, so many feelings over the last couple of days, and I can't begin to get them into an order in my head.

But on Friday Maryam told me I'd feel like this, so I think she gets it and I don't have to struggle with my words.

"OK sounds like a good start!" Maryam says with another big smile. "Are there parts of school that seem familiar?"

Yes, there are, I realise. There's Stella in Reception, the twisty stairwell in the Science block, the graffiti in the girls' loos …

"Yes," I answer simply. I don't trust those words in my head to come out of my mouth yet.

"And the other students and staff? Do you remember some of them?" Maryam asks next.

There are so many faces at school I think it would be too much to think about them all right now. So I name just one.

"There's a boy called Otis," I say, and I picture his friendly face. "He's been so kind to me."

"That's nice! And no one's upset you, have they?" Maryam checks. "You know, maybe said clumsy things about the crash. If they have, they won't *mean* to be rude. They're just curious."

Curious.

I'm pretty curious about the crash too.

The thing is, I know what happened – Mum and Dad kept a copy of the local paper to show

me. The day after the crash the headline
screamed –

LUCKY ESCAPE IN SCHOOL TRIP
COACH CRASH

It went on to say that our Year Group had
been on a field trip. We were on our way back
to school when a car came screeching out of
a side road. The coach crashed into it and
skidded 180 degrees around on the motorway.

The lucky escape was that no one in the
coach, or the car, or anyone *else* on the road
was badly hurt. Except for me.

So I know the main facts, but there's *got* to
be more.

Why did everyone else walk away with
bumps and bruises, while I ended up in hospital
with a serious head injury?

What was it like inside the coach when the crash happened?

Who helped me?

These are questions without answers.

I feel like there's stuff no one will tell me, but I don't want to ask the questions. I'm as scared as anyone else that the answers will upset me.

Chapter 4

My lucky charm

I'm doing better than anyone expected.

I mean, I don't understand a lot in lessons –
I've missed so much and my focus isn't great
yet. But I'm there, and I'm coping.

I hold onto Otis's map, and I get myself
places. That doodly map is like my lucky
charm. In fact, *he's* my lucky charm.
Yesterday (Day Three) I saw him a couple of
times at the other end of the corridor. He gave
me the widest smile, the biggest thumbs-up,
and that properly lifted my heart. It made me
feel stronger and better and braver.

Today is Day Four, and I'm still supposed to come home at the end of morning lessons. Instead, I asked Mum and Dad if I could hang around for lunch too, just to see if I'd manage. Not lunch in the noisy dining hall – lunch *out*. My Year Group are allowed out for lunch on Thursdays. Well, anyone who has good behaviour points. Adele and Urmi have told me we usually go out in a big gang, and walk up to the sandwich shop on the High Street. They say it's a total laugh.

I want to have a total laugh. I want to be carefree and silly. I want to have fun and chat and gossip.

But now that I've left my Spanish class early and I'm waiting in Reception, I'm not so sure.

"Look, maybe it's too much too soon," Stella says. She's sitting on the blue sofa beside me. She spotted me biting my nails and shivering a little bit at the idea of a big, loud crowd of girls and the big, loud, crowded High Street.

"Everything OK with Ketty?" a voice asks.

Me and Stella look up at Otis, who's holding a pile of folders.

"Ketty was supposed to go out with her friends for lunch, but she's wondering if it's a good idea or not," Stella explains as if I can't speak for myself. I suppose it's true – I feel so muddled right now I don't trust the words to come out right. Then she gets up and takes the folders from Otis.

"Do you want to come with me instead, Ketty?" Otis asks. "I'm going to have my sandwich in the park and listen to my music, since it's a nice day."

"How does that sound?" Stella asks. She's still acting as a go-between. "I could explain to your friends that you changed your mind."

"It sounds ... good," I say, and I feel the shivery bubbles of panic ebb away.

"Go on, then," Stella says, and she presses the green button to let us out. "It's not worth you going back to class for just two minutes, Otis."

Otis holds the door open for me, and his grin is as bright as the sunshine outside.

I don't know what Adele and Urmi will think about the fact I've ditched them for Otis.

But I *do* know that all of a sudden I feel the happiest I've been since I can remember, which is basically *for ever* in my case.

Chapter 5

The one I can trust

The grass in the little park next to school feels like a cool rug when we sit down on it.

"Here," Otis says, and he tears his sandwich in half. "Hope you like cheese and pickle!"

"Thanks, it's my favourite," I say, and then I slap my hand over my mouth.

"What's wrong?" he asks. His dark brown eyes are full of concern.

"No – it's great! I didn't remember that was my favourite sandwich till now!" I say with a grin.

"Does it feel good when things come back to you?" Otis asks, with a little frown.

"Yes," I assure him. "Well, most of the time. I mean, it's like finding pieces of a puzzle, which is exciting. But I don't know how they fit together, and that's kind of ..."

The word was there and now it's gone.

"Scary?" Otis suggests.

"Mmm," I say, with a shudder even though the sun is warm on my back. Even though butterflies are darting and bobbing around the nearby rose bushes.

Butterflies ...

Oh!

"Ketty?" Otis says. "Are you OK? You've gone really pale."

"I just ..." I begin, then I stop and shake my head.

It was so nearly there. As I watched the butterflies, a memory skirted so close I almost touched it.

A memory of something important.

Something about the day of the crash.

I can't bear that I didn't grab hold of it!

"Don't cry, Ketty," Otis says.

I didn't realise I was crying, till Otis reaches over as if to wipe a tear away.

But his hand brushes against my hair, and I gasp and jerk back.

Otis drops his hand.

"Sorry, did I hurt you?" he asks.

"No … it's just my hair. I don't like anyone to touch it," I say.

"Sure, OK," Otis says. He doesn't ask why, or act like I'm mad.

And then I feel bad – and at the same moment I realise I can trust him.

Trust him with the truth.

"I don't like anyone to touch it …" I start, "cos it's …"

But it's too hard to say and so, before I lose my nerve, I slip the long wig off and let him see the real me.

The stubbly dark hair that's just starting to grow after the doctors shaved it off for my operation. The vivid pink scar, the tiny bumps where the stitches were.

"Wow," Otis whispers. "Does it still hurt?"

I like the way he looks interested, not horrified.

"No, the scar's fine," I tell him. "I just get headaches sometimes."

"Y'know, with your hair that short your eyes look *amazing*," Otis says. "Really intense. Like Harley Quinn from *Suicide Squad*! Hey, maybe when it grows back, you could dye your hair white and blue and pink like hers. How cool would that be?"

Since the accident, the doctors have looked at me as a patient.

My parents have watched me like I'm made of glass.

Kids at school stare like I'm an alien.

But Otis ... Otis has just seen me at my most exposed – and compared me to the coolest movie heroine in years.

I'm so happy I could hug him – but that might be just a *bit* too weird.

Chapter 6

The key starts turning

It's Day Five, Friday.

I'm tired, but I'm nearly there. One week down, and then a weekend of quiet and rest. Dad's taken to calling me his Sleeping Beauty, since me and my recovering brain need crazy amounts of snoozing.

I'm outside Maryam the counsellor's office and Adele and Urmi have just this second walked away.

A voice calls out – "Hey, Ketty!" – and I see Otis hurrying over to me.

"Hi!" I say, grinning at my new friend.

"Listen, do you know Daisy Weston?" he asks.

I roll the name around in my mind but can't picture the face it matches.

"No, sorry," I tell him.

"Don't be sorry!" Otis says with his easy smile. "The thing is, it's Daisy's birthday tomorrow and she's decided to have a big picnic in the park to celebrate. Loads of people in our year are going."

'Not me or Adele or Urmi,' I think. We haven't been invited.

"*I'm* going, and I ... well, I just wondered if you wanted to come with me?" Otis asks.

I'm blushing. Is he asking me *out*? Or just asking me *along*? Even *my* brain knows there's a difference. A BIG difference.

"Um, yes, sure," I say, and all of a sudden I'm shy. "I better go in, I'm late for my appointment ..."

"No worries," Otis says. "How about I meet you by the café in the park at two?"

"Sure, yeah," I mumble, then I turn to knock-knock at Maryam's door.

"Are you OK, Ketty?" she asks, as soon as I'm inside. "You look a bit startled!"

"Um, I think I'm going to a sort of party tomorrow afternoon," I say as I sit down. "A big picnic for someone's birthday. With my friend Otis."

"That sounds fun," Maryam says. "Seems as if you've settled back into school life really well."

"I ... I suppose so," I reply. "But, I mean, I'm so tired, and a lot of it isn't making sense."

"Well, maybe you need to be realistic about this party. It's great to be invited, but parties can be very tiring. Are you ready for that?" Maryam asks. "I mean, only *you* know how your energy levels are."

I think for a minute, and imagine my peaceful room, my bed with its squashy duvet and soft pillows. I'd been *so* looking forward to snuggling in there for the weekend. But now?

"You don't have to rush things, Ketty," Maryam says. "You've done so well this week and you should be proud of yourself. You've taken some really big steps ..."

I start to zone out and then –

BLAM!

A picture slams into my mind. I'm standing at the top of three deep, metal steps – steps up to a coach. Outside the sun shines on a grassy meadow, and butterflies dance around. I'm standing there at the top of those steps, about to go down, and I have the most amazing sense of ... what's the word?

JOY.

That's it!

"Ketty?" Maryam says. "Are you OK?"

"It's OK," I tell her. "I just remembered something about the school trip, about the day of the crash."

It's as if a key is starting to turn a lock. A door is opening and the memories are starting to tumble out, becoming ever faster, ever clearer.

Chapter 7

The whirlwind in my head

Well, *this* is awkward.

"Nice to meet you," Dad says, and he holds out his hand for Otis to shake.

"Hi, Mr Banks," Otis says. He's acting as if the fact Dad is here isn't totally embarrassing.

"Ketty wasn't sure of the way to the café, so I had to walk her here," Dad explains to Otis, which is even *more* embarrassing.

"Sure, I get it," Otis says. "I can walk her home after the picnic, if you like?"

"Great, thanks," Dad says with a nod. "And thanks for helping out our little sweet pea this week, Otis. Ketty's mum and I really appreciate that."

No! What's Dad *doing* calling me his 'little sweet pea' in public?

I grit my teeth. "Bye, Dad," I say. "See you later."

He gets it – he goes. And now me and Otis go too, the other way.

A few minutes later, we're sitting on a picnic blanket beside a load of other people from our year.

There're sausage rolls and big bags of nachos and different types of dips. There's a tub of strawberries no one is eating, but a big box of Celebrations is gone already.

Music is blasting out from somewhere, but I can't work out where. Voices are chattering from every side, and little kids are yelping and shrieking in the playground near by.

Otis is beside me, but he's talking to Daisy, the birthday girl. I'm tuning in and out of what they're saying. There's too much background noise and I'm finding it hard to focus, but also they're talking about people and things I don't know.

"... oh, hey Otis, I got a happy birthday Snapchat from Jasmine this morning," I hear Daisy say.

'Jasmine – that's a nice name,' I think, as I pick at the skin around my nail.

And then I realise Daisy is looking at me out of the corner of her eye.

My hand goes up to check my hair – I'm always scared it'll move and people will see that it's a wig. I don't mind that Otis knows, of

course, but I don't want everyone else staring and wondering what's under it.

"Yeah? That's nice of her," Otis says. "But, hey, do you know what this track is, Daisy?"

My brain might not work 100%, but that sounded like Otis was trying to change the subject. Still, Daisy's having none of it.

"No, I don't know what it is," she says. "Anyway, Jasmine's doing great at her new school. She has lots of new friends and is really happy and chilled."

"Uh-huh, I know," Otis answers. He looks a bit uncomfortable. "Jasmine stays in touch with me too."

Jasmine.

Jasmine ...

Another flash, and a memory flits by me like a flash of brightly coloured scarf.

I expect it to go, but it doesn't. And the memory isn't a picture in my head but a twisting feeling in the pit of my stomach.

"Otis?" I say, and panic bubbles inside. "I don't feel very good!"

"OK, Ketty," Otis says. He scrambles to his feet and holds a hand out to me. "Let's go to somewhere quiet. Let's go to the roses."

The roses. The butterflies.

I get up but my head is swirling with memories and feelings like there's a whirlwind trapped inside it.

Chapter 8

Two things I know

In for five ...

Hold for five ...

Out for ten ...

With my eyes closed, I repeat my breathing exercise till the panic fades away and the whirlwind stops swirling.

"Better?" I hear Otis ask.

"Better," I say, and I open my eyes.

We're on the same grassy patch we sat on at lunch on Wednesday. This time, Otis is holding his phone in his hand instead of a sandwich. This time he has a strange expression on his face instead of a smile.

"You went a bit funny when you heard Jasmine's name, didn't you?" he says.

"Yes, but ... but I don't know why," I reply.

"Well, I think maybe I need to show you something, Ketty," he says. He looks at me and he seems a bit worried.

"Oh right," I say, frowning.

Otis turns his phone screen round so I can see.

And then I see me. Me with a girl with funky little space buns. Me scowling. Me almost growling.

"What do you think YOU'RE looking at, Jasmine?" I snarl.

The girl with the cute hair blinks hard as if she might cry.

And then it loops on again, the same little scene repeated.

And again.

"Why's it doing that, over and over?" I ask.

"It's just an app that makes five-second films," Otis says.

He looks crumpled and sad and sorry. I don't know why. I don't understand what's happening.

"Was this in Drama club?" I say. "Were we acting out a scene that you were filming?"

"It wasn't acting, Ketty," Otis says. He doesn't meet my eye. "This is you. This is how you used to be, before the crash. To lots of people, but to Jasmine most of all ..."

My brain is still bruised and I don't understand everything the way I used to, but right this second, I know two things for sure.

Otis? He's not really my friend.

And the old me? I was a *bully*. A snidey, uncaring bully.

I get up so fast my head spins, but that's the least of my worries.

I start to run.

I need to run away from here, run away from Otis, run away from myself.

Chapter 9

Tell me who I was

I only stop running when I can't breathe any longer.

My heart is hammering in my chest, my lungs burn and burn.

This part of the park ... it's wilder than the rest, it's full of long, swishing grass, like a wildflower meadow.

I sink down, or collapse, I'm not sure which.

And there are the butterflies again, darting and dancing in the soft summer breeze.

SLAM!

The memory wallops into my mind.

We had stopped at a meadow on the school trip. We gathered up our clip-boards as we got ready to file off the coach. Jasmine … she was in front of me. As I hovered at the top step by the door, Jasmine was on the next step down. It was so easy, so tempting. I nudged her in the back and she tumbled forward, all the way out of the coach. She crumpled down onto the road, hitting her bare knees on the gritty surface.

And I felt elated, full of JOY.

"Ketty – Ketty, I'm so sorry," Otis pants, and I feel him flop down beside me in the long grass.

"Don't be," I say. I stare at him, and my eyes stream with tears. "Just tell me. Tell me the truth. I know you hate me, but please tell me who I was."

Otis sighs, and he stares at the ground as he talks.

"Jasmine tried a couple of times to tell teachers that you were bullying her, but you were smart and popular and you always convinced them it was all lies. Jasmine was my friend, so I filmed you in secret whenever you were near her. I wanted to catch you out. But even when I had this clip, Jasmine told me I was wasting my time – her mum had got a job in London, and they were moving away. Jasmine just wanted a fresh start, to be happy, to feel safe at school."

"And I made her miserable," I say. My voice is flat. "She must have hated me. I hate myself right now. Was I really that bad?"

"Uh, pretty much," Otis says. He holds his phone screen up for me to see again. I flinch away from it – is it another of those films?

It's me again, that's for sure. It looks like the inside of a coach. I'm standing on the seat, reaching into a bag on the shelf above.

"Sit down, Ketty Banks!" a voice shouts. It must belong to a teacher.

"Oh, shut up! I just need my lip gloss!" I growl in reply.

Then there's an awful thud, and the phone clatters to the ground while the sound of screaming fills the coach.

Otis presses pause before the loop begins again.

"So *that's* why I ended up with such a bad injury, compared to everyone else," I say. "In a way, it was my own stupid fault!"

I stare at the frozen image on the screen in horror. Mum and Dad might think I'm the same girl I was, but that's just not true. And I'm *glad*.

"Look, Ketty," Otis says, "I've been a bit confused lately. I – I – hated the old Ketty, and so I got close to you this week cos I wanted to … I dunno, hurt you like you hurt Jasmine, drive you away like you did her. But the trouble is …"

He stops. I look up at him, and I know my face is a messy sea of tears and snot.

"… the trouble is, I really, REALLY like the new Ketty." He bites his lip.

Otis – he made me feel brave this week.

And all of a sudden I feel brave again.

I reach out my fingers and touch his hand.

"I really, REALLY like the new me too," I whisper.

As Otis wraps his fingers around mine, I feel so, *so* glad that the old Ketty 'died' in those two minutes, 39 seconds on the day of the school trip.

Because, even with my bruises and my scars and my fuzzy, messed-up head, I'm the new, improved Ketty – and I'm here to stay.

Our books are tested
for children and young people by
children and young people.

Thanks to everyone who consulted on
a manuscript for their time and effort in
helping us to make our books better
for our readers.